Slime Time

Want more books by Debbie Dadey?
Then check out . . .

Swamp Monster in Third Grade

Swamp Monster in Third Grade #2: *Lizards in the Lunch Line*

The Slime Wars

And don't forget . . .

The Adventures of
THE
BAILEY SCHOOL
KIDS®

Ghostville
Elementary®

by Debbie Dadey and Marcia Thornton Jones

Slime Time

by Debbie and Nathan Dadey

Illustrated by
Bill Basso

A
LITTLE APPLE
PAPERBACK

SCHOLASTIC INC.

NEW YORK   TORONTO   LONDON   AUCKLAND   SYDNEY
MEXICO CITY   NEW DELHI   HONG KONG   BUENOS AIRES

To Eric, Becky, and Alex Dadey —
with love —ND and DD

No part of this publication may be reproduced in whole or in part, stored in a retrieval system, or transmitted in any form or by any means, electronic, mechanical, photocopying, recording, or otherwise, without written permission of the publisher. For information regarding permission, write to Scholastic Inc., Attention: Permissions Department, 557 Broadway, New York, NY 10012.

ISBN 0-439-64362-7

Text copyright © 2004 by Debra S. Dadey and Nathan Dadey.
Illustrations copyright © 2003 by Scholastic Inc.
SCHOLASTIC, LITTLE APPLE, and associated logos are trademarks and/or registered trademarks of Scholastic Inc.

12 11 10 9 8 7 6 5 4 3 2 1   4 5 6 7 8 9/0

Printed in the U.S.A.   40
First printing, May 2004

CONTENTS

Chapter 1
TERRIBLE TRIO

There's a line down the middle of our street. Some people think it's for car lanes, but I know better. It's the dividing line. Patrick, Will, and I live on the south side of Daleside Drive: the boys' side. We live a few houses away from one another. The girls live on the north side. Tammy and Karen are sisters and Angela is their next-door neighbor. Anyone who steps over the line is looking for trouble. The war between the boys and the girls of Daleside Drive had been going on for as long as I could remember. Every so often it would get really bad.

That's what happened this fall — the terrible trio came cruising for trouble and things got bad. Patrick, Will, and I were minding our own business, playing basketball in my driveway, when it all started.

"Two points!" Will shouted as the ball swished through the net. He took off his baseball cap and tossed it in the air in a victory dance.

"Easy for you," Patrick said. "If I was eight feet tall, I could swish basketballs all day long, too." Will is the tallest of the three of us and outweighs us by ten pounds, so he always manages to beat us at basketball — but that doesn't stop us from trying.

"Yeah, and if you and Justin were ugly, you could be two of the girls," Will teased us.

"Speaking of ugly," Patrick said, "here comes the terrible trio."

"Oh, no," I groaned. "Trouble at twelve o'clock." Tammy the Terrible led her sister, Karen, and their friend Angela across the street. I could tell by the way Tammy's long blond hair swung from side to side and by the frown on her face that this wasn't going to be a happy visit.

"What do you want?" Patrick snapped.

2

"We want our computer," Tammy demanded, putting her hands on her hips.

"Oh, no," I groaned again. The computer hadn't even been delivered yet and there was already trouble. Last summer, all six of us had been on a TV game show called *The Slime Wars*. We'd lost, but we had still gotten some pretty good prizes, like a computer to split between the six of us.

Will threw the basketball toward Tammy, but she ducked just in time. "No, I don't think so!" he shouted. "When the computer comes, we get it. After all, it was Justin's idea to be on the game show, so we should have it first."

"What kind of crappy contest just gives away one computer, anyway?" Tammy snapped.

"Well, we did each get a new bike," Patrick said quietly.

I knew Patrick felt bad enough already. He was the one who answered the last question wrong on the game show. After that, our team fell into a huge slime pit.

"We would have each won a computer if you hadn't messed us up," Karen told Patrick.

"We were all on the team," I said. "It's not Patrick's fault we lost."

"We need that computer," Karen said, tossing blond curls back off her face. "We're going to use it to get ready for the school carnival." Every year, our school has a carnival, and kids are assigned a booth. All the money earned goes to the school to pay for after-school programs, but the kids whose booth makes the most money get a limo ride to Fun Zone, with unlimited games for a whole afternoon.

"That's a load of micropoop," said Patrick. "You're just going to use the computer for some girly stuff."

"No," Tammy said, "we're going to use it to make signs for our booth. I heard Paula Dimsey is going to have her signs professionally made at Kinko's."

"Don't you mean Paula Dimwitty?" Will teased. He stuck his nose up in the air and

pretended to be Paula. "I have more money than the U.S. Treasury," he said, prancing around on his tiptoes.

"You shouldn't tease her," Angela said. "I think Paula is nice." All the kids turned to Angela in surprise. No one had ever used the words *nice* and *Paula* in the same sentence.

"Well," Angela said with a red face, "I'm sure she's nice if you get to know her."

"She's so stuck-up, she doesn't know where the planet Earth is," Patrick said.

"We need the computer because our booth is going to be the best," I told the girls.

"If you don't let us have the computer, you'll be sorry," Tammy snapped.

Chapter 2
SPLAT!

"This is awesome," Will said as he blasted into hyperspace to avoid being killed by Bombardo. Then *blam*! "Rats, I just got wasted, but I made it through level four."

Patrick pushed Will out of the way and took a turn at the new computer. It had been delivered only two hours ago, and already we had played forty-seven games of Destructo Bombardo. Since Will had the only computer desk at his house, that's where we had set it up. "We should keep this computer forever," Will said, "and never share with the girls. What could they do about it?"

I shuddered. The girls could do a lot of things, like throwing tennis balls with rotten eggs in them or putting Vaseline in my in-line skates. They had done those things before, and I didn't want to find out what they'd think up next.

"Let's see if we can look up any ideas for our carnival booth," I suggested.

Patrick moaned. "No, I'm almost to the asteroid field on level five. Look at that alien mother ship!"

"Sweet," Will said, hanging over Patrick's shoulder to get a closer look at the glowing seventeen-inch, flat-panel screen.

Blam-bam! "Oh, man. I just got blasted into teeny tiny little pieces!" Patrick said.

I shoved Patrick out of the computer chair and looked up carnival games on the Internet. "Let's see what we can do to win the day at Fun Zone." A few clicks later, we found a cool site that listed a bunch of ideas for carnival games.

"No way," Will said, pointing at the screen. "Face painting is lame."

Patrick laughed. "We did a duck pond in preschool."

"What about a dunking booth?" I suggested.

I looked at Patrick and Will. They both looked at me and smiled.

"Cool," Will said. "I think we've got some stuff in my garage we could use."

Will's garage smelled like sawdust mixed with pickles. The sawdust was from his dad's furniture projects, and the pickle smell was left over from the time Will dropped a five-gallon jar of dill pickles, brand-new from Sam's Club. Besides the smell, the garage was like a treasure chest. Every nook and cranny bulged with old tires, power tools, and plywood.

Will dragged out an old washtub. "We could use this," he suggested.

"Maybe we could balance this old chair on the edge somehow," I said, knocking dust off a rickety old kitchen chair.

We worked on the dunking booth for at least twenty minutes, but all we ended up doing was getting sore from falling off the chair. "Man, this is too hard," Patrick said. "Let's try something else."

"How about a dart-throwing booth?" Will

suggested, grabbing a rusty dart from an old target in the garage. "We could use this one."

"Great idea," I said. "We could pin up some balloons and pop them with the darts."

"Yeah, maybe people could win prizes," Patrick said.

Will ran into the house. "I'll be right back," he called. He came back a minute later with a heap of multicolored balloons.

"Now we're talking," I said, spreading the balloons on the garage floor. Things were beginning to shape up. I could just picture myself in that limo heading toward Fun Zone.

We were hunched over the balloons when trouble came calling. "It's payback time!" Tammy yelled.

Splat! Pow! Bam-o! A balloon filled with green slime splatted me on the chest. Will got plastered in the face with slime.

"You stupid girls!" Patrick screamed with green goo dripping off his nose.

"You got us slimed on TV, now it's our

turn," laughed Karen, holding up a video camera. She had filmed us getting our faces splattered.

Then the girls sped off on their bikes, leaving our carnival plans knee-deep in slime.

Chapter 3
RUINED

"They're ruined!" Will yelled and kicked at our slime-soaked balloons on the floor of the garage. Green goo splattered all over his jeans.

"Maybe we could wash off our balloons," I suggested.

Patrick held up a slimy orange balloon. Big blobs of green ooze dripped off it and plopped onto the garage floor. "I don't want to wash it," he said. "Those girls probably used toxic toilet water to make this slime."

The slime did smell pretty bad. I tried to wipe it off my Chicago Bulls jersey. If those girls had ruined my souvenir Michael Jordan #23 shirt, they were going to be in big trouble. Still, I didn't want us getting into a war over this. I wanted to make peace. "I've got some allowance left. Let's buy more balloons at the mall this weekend."

Will spit slime out of his mouth and wiped his face with his sleeve. "Sure, we can get new balloons, but those girls will still have to pay."

Patrick's face glowed, and I knew we were in trouble. "What do you have in mind?" he asked. There was nothing Patrick liked better than playing tricks on people. Once he had put itching powder in my underwear — and I'm his *friend.* You can just imagine what he'd do to someone who had just thrown slime at him.

"Public humiliation," said Will. "That's the way to get them back. The bigger, the better."

"This week's school assembly for the carnival is perfect," said Patrick. Their words gave me a sick feeling in my stomach that had nothing to do with toxic toilet water slime.

Three days later at the assembly, I still had that sick feeling in my stomach. "This year's carnival will be the best ever," Principal Barbo told us, "as long as we remember one simple rule. Nothing dangerous, such as sharp points."

Will and Patrick both groaned on the bleachers beside me. That rule meant no dart throwing.

"Oh, well," I whispered. "We'll just have to think of something that's even *better*."

"This will cheer you up," Patrick told us softly. He pulled a small black-and-white book out of his jeans pocket.

"What's that?" Will asked. We ducked our heads down so Principal Barbo wouldn't see us talking.

"It's Tammy's diary," Patrick said, grinning mischievously. His evil villain laugh made me feel almost sorry for Tammy.

"How did you get her diary?" I whispered.

"I didn't," Patick said. "I made the whole thing up. But no one else needs to know that. I used my best handwriting."

The sick feeling in my stomach got

stronger and stronger. I flipped open the diary and read:

Dear Diary, I am so in love with Bart Middleton, I can hardly stand it. Tammy

I flipped to another page.

Dear Diary, Paula Dimsey is a jerk. She wears stupid clothes, too. Tammy

"Come on," I told Patrick, "we can't do this."

"Oh, yes, we can," Will said. He jerked the diary out of my hands and tossed it over to a big group of boys. One of them was Bart Middleton.

There was a lot of laughing and giggling as the diary was passed from group to group. It wasn't long before I heard Tammy's scream.

Unfortunately, Principal Barbo heard it, too.

Chapter 4
DEATH ROW

That's how we ended up in Principal Barbo's office, with three girls on one side and three boys on the other. Principal Barbo sat in the middle, drumming her fingers on her desk. Tammy's made-up diary sat between us on the desk.

"There's only one thing to do," Principal Barbo said firmly.

"Apologize?" Angela said softly.

I held my breath. Could we really get off that easy? This was my first visit to the principal's office, and I wasn't enjoying the experience at all.

"Good idea," Principal Barbo said. I let out my breath with a big sigh. But I had sighed too soon.

"Also," Principal Barbo continued. I

looked at Will and Patrick in terror. What was she going to do to us?

"I think it's time you six got over this childishness and learned to cooperate with one another," Principal Barbo said. "Your teachers have told me this isn't the first time you've had problems."

I hung my head in embarrassment and wondered if Principal Barbo was going to call my mom. I'd be grounded for the rest of my life.

"You need to be disciplined," Principal Barbo said.

I gulped and sweat trickled down my forehead. Will and Patrick wiggled in their chairs. Tammy looked mad, but Angela and Karen were pale. I figured Karen would throw up at any moment.

Principal Barbo stood up and handed down her punishment. "You three boys and you three girls will have a booth *together* at the carnival. It seems that being together is worse punishment than a month's worth of detention."

"No," Tammy gasped, raising her hand to her mouth in horror.

"You can start by eating lunch together and coming up with an idea for the booth." Principal Barbo looked at her watch. "You may head to the cafeteria now."

We walked out the door like death-row inmates. In one sentence, Principal Barbo had ruined any chance for fun at the carnival. And what about winning the day at Fun Zone? We could kiss that good-bye, too.

"This is all your fault!" Tammy snapped when we were far enough away from the principal's office.

"Our fault?" Patrick said. "Who started the whole thing by throwing slime at us?"

"Thanks to you," Will said, "the best part of the whole year is ruined!"

"Maybe it won't be so bad," I said as we headed into the cafeteria.

Paula Dimsey pushed past us just as we walked in. "Hellllllllllooooo," she chortled. "Something stinks in the lunchroom — and it isn't the food." She giggled at her own lame joke and pranced off toward the salad bar.

"You know," Tammy said, "I didn't write that Paula was a jerk in my diary, but if I had a diary I would have written worse stuff than that."

"One of these days we'll find a way to shut her up," Will vowed as we went through the lunch line.

Chapter 5
CREAMED TURKEY

Will slammed his tray full of creamed turkey onto the cafeteria table. I ducked to avoid little pieces of splattering gravy. "I can't believe we have to sit with those girls," he complained.

"Let's just get this over with," Patrick said, slumping down on the bench.

"Having to sit with those girls made me lose my appetite," Will said as he woofed down a huge portion of creamed turkey and mashed potatoes.

Angela, Tammy, and Karen put their trays on the table across from us. "How can you eat that sludge?" Karen asked Will.

Potatoes dripped out of Will's mouth as he shoved in another spoonful of turkey.

"Ugh, that's disgusting," Tammy said, trying to ignore him.

"You should see him when he's *really* hungry," Patrick said.

"Let's just figure out what we're going to do for the carnival," I suggested.

Paula Dimsey walked by with her tiny salad and bottle of water. "You clowns should forget about the carnival. *I* am going to have the best booth and *I* am going to win the prize."

Tammy's face turned the same bright pink as her T-shirt. "We'll have the best booth," she said, "and we'll make your puny booth look like a two-year-old made it."

"In your dreams," Paula sniffed. "My big sister, Leslie, is helping me and my friends. You morons don't stand a chance."

"Your big sister is just as stuck-up as you are," Patrick yelled.

Paula giggled. "That's not what your big brother thinks."

Patrick's ears turned red. "So what?" he sputtered. "We'll still beat you."

"Want to bet?" Paula said.

"Yeah," Karen said, jumping to Patrick's defense. "We'll bet you our dessert every day for a month." At our school, lunch was made by the hairnet-wearing Lupin twins. Those ladies took delight in making our food look like slop. The desserts were the only thing that made lunch bearable.

Paula's eyes flashed and she hesitated for just a second.

"Afraid you'll lose?" Angela asked.

"No," Paula snapped. "It's a deal. My friends and I will enjoy your desserts next month." Paula flounced off toward a table of Paula look-alikes.

"You DO have a plan for our booth, right?" Karen asked Tammy.

Tammy shook her head slowly. "I have no idea."

Will couldn't believe it. "You mean, you girls just bet my dessert, and you don't even have a plan?" He took his carrot cake and tossed it at Tammy.

Tammy ducked and the carrot cake skidded across the tile floor, leaving a trail of white icing. Tammy picked up her full lunch tray and aimed it at Will. "You're going to get it now, buddy."

I grabbed Tammy's tray before Will got creamed with salad dressing. "Wait!" I said. "You just gave me the perfect idea!"

Chapter 6
PERFECT PINK PIES

Tammy put her tray down on the cafeteria table, but she kept her fingers clenched on the edges. "What's your idea?" she snapped at me. "If it's not good, you're *all* getting a faceful of salad."

I gulped, and Patrick patted me on the back. "Go ahead, Justin. I have half a plate of potatoes left. If Tammy tries anything, I'll make sure she gets it first."

Tammy tossed back her hair and gave me a look that would shred metal. "My idea," I said hoarsely, "is a pie-throwing booth."

No one said a word. I squinted, afraid that Tammy was going to send her lunch my way. Nothing happened. Silence.

Then Will and Patrick smiled. Tammy, Karen, and Angela looked at one another

and shrugged. "I guess that's okay," Tammy said slowly.

"I like it," Karen said, and I breathed a sigh of relief. "We can make a booth and paint it pink."

"We could wear little pink aprons that say *Perfect Pies*," Angela suggested.

Will spit out his last bite of turkey. "No way!" he snapped. "We're not going to wear aprons — ever."

I put my hand up in the air. "The girls can wear aprons if they want, we don't have to."

"My brother, Ralph, can help us make the booth," Patrick suggested.

I nodded. Patrick's older brother was pretty cool. He had even shown us how to beat level three in Destructo Bombardo.

Will pushed his tray away and jumped up. "There's no way we're going to have a pink booth."

Tammy stood up from the table. "The booth will be pink if we want it to be pink."

"Over my dead body," Will said, standing up and glaring at Tammy.

"That can be arranged," Tammy said seriously.

I pulled Will's arm and Angela tugged on Tammy's. "Let's calm down," I said.

"What about the pies?" Patrick asked.

"What are you talking about?" Tammy snapped at Patrick.

"Well, someone is going to have to get hit in the face with them," he said. "And it's not going to be me."

"I'm not doing it," Karen squealed.

"Yuck," Angela said.

"Everyone will have to do it," I said. "It's only fair."

Now Tammy held up her hand. "We'll get the pies in the face on one condition."

"What?" Karen and Angela squealed at the same time.

Tammy nodded. "We'll take the pies in the face if you give us the computer this month *and* next month."

"All right," Patrick said immediately.

"Not so fast," Will said. "You also have to do our math homework *every day*."

"I don't think so," Karen said.

"Wait just a second," Tammy said. She stopped and winked at her friends, then nodded. "We'll do it."

I couldn't believe it. Tammy must have really wanted that computer. Things were finally going my way.

"All right," Patrick agreed. "After school, you can have the computer."

Will laughed. "I can't wait to see you guys get a faceful of pie."

"And no math homework for a whole month," I said with a grin. Things couldn't have been better.

I should have known that my luck wouldn't last.

Chapter 7
MISSING

"What did you do with it?" Tammy screeched.

"It was right here," Patrick said. He had a strange green tinge to his face, like he was going to be sick. I felt a little sick, too. The computer was missing. Only a layer of dust remained on the computer desk. All six of us stared at the empty desk — boys on one side and girls on the other.

"You're lying," Karen said. "You just don't want us to use the computer so you *hid* it."

"We don't want you to have it," Will said. "In fact, we'd love it if you'd just fall off the face of the earth. But we didn't hide the computer."

Will looked under the desk and behind Patrick's bedroom door. I threw Patrick's bedspread up in the air. Patrick pulled open his closet door and a box of baseball cards fell off the top shelf. Cards scattered all over the floor. Patrick kicked them aside and rummaged through his closet.

"Look," I explained. "We just got home from school. We didn't have time to hide anything."

Angela put her arms across her chest and stared at me. "Then where is it?"

"You don't think someone stole it, do you?" Will asked.

I shrugged. The thought had crossed my mind. "No," Patrick said. "My mom's been here all day."

"If you don't find that computer," Tammy said, pointing her finger at Will, "you'll be the one getting all the pies in the face."

"It's worse than that," Will yelled. "If we don't find the computer, I'll never get to play Destructo Bombardo ever again!"

"It's got to be in the house somewhere," Patrick said. "Let's keep looking."

"All right," I said. "Let's start in the basement and work our way up." That seemed

logical to me, so we wouldn't miss any rooms.

In the basement, Will and Angela took a few minutes to play Ping-Pong before Tammy screamed at them, "Come on, this isn't a party. This is serious."

We peeked into every closet and under every bed in Patrick's whole house. Even his mother was baffled.

"Maybe one of our moms borrowed it," I suggested to Will. It didn't seem very likely, but I didn't know what else to say. Computers didn't just disappear.

Tammy poked me in the chest. "You'd better hope your mom has it," she said, "or I'll tell Paula Dimsey that you love her." Angela put her hand over her mouth to stifle a giggle.

I gulped. "You wouldn't dare."

"Oh, wouldn't I?" Tammy said as the girls left Will's house.

Chapter 8
PIE TIME

"It's gone," Will moaned. We had looked everywhere for the flat-screen monitor and brand-new computer, but it was hopeless. We had even looked in Patrick's doghouse. No luck. Now we were sprawled under the big tree in front of Will's house.

"The girls are going to kill us," Patrick moaned, tossing some leaves up in the air. One floated down and landed on my chest.

I nodded. I hoped Tammy hadn't been serious about telling Paula Dimsey that I loved her. Otherwise, the rest of sixth grade would be a major nightmare.

"Maybe we can get their minds off the computer," Patrick suggested. "At least until we find it."

"How are we going to do that?" I asked.

"Watch and learn," Patrick said as the girls crossed the street toward us.

Before Tammy had a chance to say a word, Patrick jumped up. "I have an awesome idea," he said.

"It better have something to do with us getting the computer," Tammy snapped, "or you're dead."

"No problem," Patrick said. "But first, we have to make pies for the booth."

I could tell the girls hadn't thought about that. "Oh, that's right," Angela said with a giggle.

"We can use my kitchen," Will suggested. "My mom won't care."

Last summer, Will's mom had let us make brownies for the girls. That was when we were trying to bribe them into being on the game show with us.

"Let's do it," Tammy said.

It took some fast talking, but Will's mom agreed to let us use her kitchen as long as we promised to clean up our mess.

"First, we need lots of flour," Tammy said.

Will pulled a five-pound paper bag of flour out of the pantry and tossed it at Tammy. Unfortunately, it hit the counter instead of Tammy and detonated like a hand grenade. *POW*! White powder exploded everywhere.

"Jerk-face!" Tammy yelled. "See what you did?"

"Why didn't you catch it?" Will yelled back. "Look at the mess you made."

Patrick laughed and pointed at Tammy. She was coated in white powder from her pink hair bow all the way down to her matching tennis shoes.

"You're like Casper the friendly ghost — only without the friendly part," Patrick said.

I knew that to be true, because Tammy's face was anything but friendly.

Karen and Angela giggled, but they stopped as soon as Tammy glared at them. "You moron, now we don't even have the flour to make the pies," she said to Will, wiping white dust off her arms.

"No problem," Will said. He grabbed a dustpan and started scooping.

"You can't make pies with dirty flour," Karen told him.

"Why not?" Patrick said. "It's not like anyone's going to eat them."

"And besides," Will said, "my mom just mopped the floor last week."

"Ewww," Angela said.

Tammy just groaned and shook her head. Flour sprinkled to the floor like snowflakes. "Let's make these pies before you guys drive me crazy."

Will opened a cabinet and took out a cookbook while I finished sweeping the flour into a dustpan. I tried to pick out the hairs and dirt clumps.

Karen read the choices. "Apple, banana cream, cherry, chocolate cream . . ."

"Oh, man," Will groaned. "This is making me hungry."

"Look," Patrick said. "That sounds like a lot of work. All we really need is something to throw. Something that looks like a pie."

"I guess so," Angela said slowly.

Patrick popped open the refrigerator door

and pulled out some jars. Into a pie pan he poured flour, some dill pickles, and a container of vanilla pudding. Over the pudding he squirted chocolate syrup.

"We can't use that," Tammy said. "It's disgusting! Paula Dimsey will laugh at us."

"Who cares about Paula Dimsey?" Will said. "We're just going to throw it."

"We have to beat Paula," Karen said. "Her booth will probably be perfect."

"That looks like slime," Angela moaned.

Will shoved the weird pie toward Angela. It sloshed onto her shirt. "Does it feel like slime?" he asked.

Angela grabbed a handful of vanilla pudding and flung it in Will's face. "How's this for slime?" she yelled.

That's when I dove for cover under the kitchen table. Food soared all over the room.

Patrick slipped on pickle juice and landed beside me. He licked his fingers. "It's slime time!"

Chapter 9
STINKERS

"Those look good enough to eat," Will said, grabbing one of the pies the girls had made. It was the day of the carnival, and the playground swarmed with people setting up their booths.

Tammy slapped Will's hand. "Those are for throwing, NOT eating," she said.

The girls had made their own pies, and they looked delicious. It seemed a shame to waste perfectly good eating pies on throwing, but it had to be done.

Pies weren't the only thing the girls had done on their own. They had spray-painted a big wooden box red with a yellow top for their side of the booth. Our side was a big toilet paper box that Will had found behind the Piggly Wiggly grocery store. Patrick's

43

brother had been too busy to help us make a wooden box, so we made do with cardboard. The girls had painted GIRLS' PIE TOSS in big yellow letters on their box, and STINKERS in big green letters on ours. I didn't say a word when I saw STINKERS. I quickly covered it up with a poster I had made out of a brown paper bag before Will and Patrick could see it. I wrote SLIME TIME on the bag in big black letters.

The girls had folding tables for their pies, but ours just sat in the grass. We had run out of pie tins, so most of our pies were on soggy paper plates. All of the girls' were in proper pie tins. I wondered where they had scrounged up so many. They had at least thirty good-looking pies.

Our pies might not have looked very good, but they were fun to throw. "Get your slime pies here." Will yelled. Boys from pre-schoolers to grandpas lined up behind our toilet paper box to throw their pies at Patrick. The girls frowned and watched.

Patrick made a fun target. His face stuck

through a hole we had cut out of a big refrigerator box. He had a bull's-eye target painted on his face and he yelled insults at everyone. "You couldn't hit your dog if it was peeing on you!"

Bam! Principal Barbo paid three dollars to try to hit Patrick. Every pie fell short. "Missed me. Missed me," Patrick screamed. "Now you gotta pay me."

Every one of Patrick's teachers lined up to try to hit him. *Bam. Bam. Bam.* None of them had any luck, until Coach Cady stepped up.

A huge crowd gathered around. "Look, Coach," Patrick squealed. "I'm sorry about last Friday. I didn't know that ugly lady was your wife!"

Splat! Patrick got it right in the mouth! The crowd around our booth cheered for Coach Cady.

"Bleech!" Patrick spit a pudding-covered pickle out of his mouth. "Maybe those pickles weren't such a good idea, after all," he said.

After Patrick got hit, things slowed down a little. We had made tons of money with our icky pies. I just hoped it was enough to win the trip to Fun Zone.

"Your booth looks like it was made by a baboon," Paula Dimsey said snidely as she walked by. "Your letters aren't even straight." Then she flounced back to her paper-flower-making booth, but not before flashing me a smile. Had Tammy made good on her threat of telling Paula that I loved her?

"Our booth does look stupid," Tammy hissed at us boys. "And it's all your fault."

"Hey, if it wasn't for us, you wouldn't have made any money," Will said, holding up a fistful of dollars. It was true. Most of our slime pies were gone, and the girls still had plenty of their good-looking pies left.

Patrick hopped out from behind the refrigerator box. "If I'm going to get hit with all these pies, I should get to eat one." Patrick picked up a banana cream pie just as Tammy grabbed the other side of it. They pulled back and forth on the pie.

"Give it to me!" Patrick yelled.

Tammy smiled and said, "Okay." She let

go and the pie slammed Patrick right in the face.

"Oh, you're going to get it now," Patrick yelled, picking up another pie. Will got into the act and tossed a pie right at Tammy's head.

"Stop!" Angela screamed at Patrick. "We need these pies for the booth." Angela got in the way of Patrick's toss and ended up with pie all over her T-shirt.

"You asked for it!" Karen yelled. She threw a strawberry pie right at Patrick. He ducked and the pie got me right in the chest.

I licked the strawberry filling off my T-shirt. Yummm. It tasted great.

"Take that," Tammy yelled. "You and your stupid pie-throwing booth." She hit me right in the mouth with a rhubarb pie.

I licked my lips and yelled, "It's not stupid if we beat Paula Dimsey." Tammy put down a peach pie as an evil grin crossed her face.

Chapter 10
MYSTERY GUEST

"What did I say?" I asked Will and Patrick.

"Who cares?" Patrick said, licking whipped cream off his face. "They're gone."

The girls had whispered and giggled. Then Tammy announced, "We're going to get you lots of customers, so don't eat up the pies."

Will nodded, but as soon as the girls were out of sight, he bit into a delicious-looking butterscotch pie. Patrick and I grabbed a hunk of pie for ourselves. We were still smacking our lips when a huge line began to form in front of our toilet paper box.

"Want to throw a pie at Patrick?" I asked with butterscotch still in my mouth.

Two girls in the front of the line giggled and shook their heads. "No, we're waiting for the mystery guest."

The line got longer and longer, but no one wanted to throw a pie at Will, or Patrick, or even me. They all waited for the special mystery guest.

"Who's the mystery guest?" Will asked.

I shrugged. No one would tell us; everyone just smiled and waited.

Finally, Tammy, Karen, and Angela rushed back up to our booth. "What is going on?" Patrick asked.

"Practically the whole school is lined up for some mystery guest," I told the girls. "Who are they talking about?"

"Shhh," Tammy said.

"What's going on over here?" Paula Dimsey asked, walking up to the girls. I could tell she was jealous of our huge crowd.

"Thank you, Paula, for coming to visit our booth," Angela said sweetly.

Patrick, Will, and I stared at Angela. What was going on?

"Your booth is the worst one here," Paula snipped. "Mine is much better."

"Humph," Patrick said.

Paula looked Patrick right in the eye and said, "Thanks for letting me borrow your new computer. It made such nice signs for my carnival booth. I'm sure I'll win."

"What?" Will, Patrick, and I said together.

Paula smiled. "Oh, Patrick, didn't your big brother tell you he lent your computer to my sister?"

So that's what had happened to our computer. We all stood there openmouthed while Paula turned to go.

"Wait," Will said. "I want to give you a pie for free."

Will did, all right. He popped her right in the face with a slime pie! Paula shrieked and Tammy grabbed her.

"Thanks for helping us," Karen said as she helped Tammy pull Paula behind their pink booth.

"What?" Paula said, still dazed from the pie in her face.

Before Paula could say *boo*, the kids in line were stepping up to slam pies into her face. It was Slime Time and *Paula* was our

mystery guest! It made sense. Everyone would want to smash her in the face with pie. We raked in ten dollars before Paula shrieked, "You guys are going to be in so much trouble when Principal Barbo finds out about this!"

Paula stormed back over to her own booth with slime and strawberries caked in her hair. Paula look-alikes surrounded her and wiped off her face.

"You know we might get into big trouble over that," I told my booth coworkers.

Will smiled. "It doesn't matter," he said. "It was worth it."

Patrick, Angela, Tammy, Karen, Will, and I laughed. For once, we all agreed on something.

Chapter 11
THE WINNERS

"And the winners of the day at Fun Zone are . . ." Principal Barbo paused and everyone in the gym held their breath.

"Please," Patrick said, closing his eyes and crossing his fingers.

Principal Barbo continued, "Will Simon, Patrick Brown, and Justin O'Reilly . . ."

Will, Patrick, and I stood up and cheered. Patrick did a victory dance on the stairs, but he stopped dancing when Principal Barbo finished.

". . . along with Karen and Tammy Rynearson and Angela Fielding for their pie-throwing booth." On the other side of the gym, Karen, Tammy, and Angela screamed.

Patrick and Will groaned. "You mean, we

have to share our prize with them . . . *again*?"

I shrugged. "They *did* get Paula for us to slime." And, after Paula had gotten pied, the girls made even more money by selling the rest of their pies to the teachers to eat.

We all ran down to the podium. Tammy beat us and grabbed the microphone. "We want to especially thank Paula Dimsey for her help," Tammy announced. All the kids in the assembly cheered, and Paula stormed out of the gym.

"That was very kind of Paula," Principal Barbo said. "That's probably what she wanted to talk to me about earlier."

"Probably," I said as I took my Fun Zone certificate.

"Look, Justin, no hands!" Patrick screamed. We were on the Typhoon roller coaster at Fun Zone. Patrick and I shared a car. Karen and Tammy were behind us. Will shared with Angela since she was scared to go alone.

The roller coaster jerked and went into two barrel rolls. "AAAAAAHHHH!" we screamed as we flew through the last turn and slammed to a stop.

Behind us I could hear Karen gagging. Patrick didn't get out of the car fast enough, and Karen threw up all over his back.

"Oh, I'm so sorry," Karen moaned.

Patrick took off his jacket and tossed it at Karen. "Here's your souvenir from Fun Zone. Don't say I didn't ever give you anything."

Karen recovered enough to get in the bumper cars. She still looked a little queasy, though. I tried to stay away from her.

Tammy got in a bright pink bumper car. "It's still our turn for the computer," she yelled.

"Too late," Will said. "The carnival is over, and Patrick took all the pies in the face."

"Except the ones that Paula got," Angela said with a giggle. The bumper cars sparked to life and we took off.

"It is, too, our turn!" Tammy screamed.

Patrick chased after Karen in his green bumper car. "You'll get that computer when we're good and ready," he said.

"And after you've done all our math homework," Will added.

I mashed the pedal on my car and bumped into Tammy. She turned and gave me an icy glare. I could tell that the war between the boys and the girls of Daleside Drive wasn't over yet.

ABOUT THE AUTHORS

Debbie Dadey is the author and coauthor of more than one hundred children's books, including *The Adventures of the Bailey School Kids* and *Ghostville Elementary* series. Debbie lives in Fort Collins, Colorado, with her family and two dogs. Nathan Dadey is Debbie's teenage son, and this is his second book. The *Slime Time* idea came from a backyard carnival to benefit the Humane Society. The pie-throwing was a big hit!

Ready for some spooky fun?
Then take a sneak peek
at the new series from
Marcia Thornton Jones
and Debbie Dadey!

Ghostville Elementary®

#5 Stage Fright

Finally, at two o'clock in the afternoon, Mr. Morton cleared his throat. "Okay, class," he announced. "It's time for the play auditions."

A few kids groaned, but most kids cheered. Carla and Darla clapped their hands. Everyone put away their spelling worksheets and took out their copy of the book the class had been reading together.

"Remember, each part is important," Mr. Morton told the class. "And we will need many students to make the set and decorations for the play."

"Now, let's see who is interested in playing Travis?" Mr. Morton asked. Jeff, Andrew, and Cassidy raised their hands in the air.

Jeff looked at Andrew. "I thought you didn't like plays," Jeff said.

Andrew shrugged. "I thought I'd give it a try."

Andrew went first. Jeff had to admit that Andrew was pretty good. Cassidy went next and read her part out loud. Jeff sank down in his seat. Cassidy was really good, too.

When Mr. Morton called his name, Jeff walked slowly to the front of the room. Jeff turned his book to page six and opened his mouth. Nothing came out. Jeff stood frozen to the floor like time had stopped.

"What's wrong with Jeff?" Nina whispered to Cassidy.

Cassidy didn't say anything, either. She just pointed. When Nina saw what Cassidy was pointing at, Nina froze, too. . . .

Jeff stared at a strange figure hovering in the back corner of the room. It was a girl dressed in a flowing white gown. Her long dark hair floated above her head as she bowed slightly at Jeff.

Of course, only Jeff, Cassidy, and Nina could see her. The rest of the class, including their teacher, didn't realize a new ghost was in their midst.

"Jeff? Jeff?" Mr. Morton asked. "Are you okay?"

Jeff's mouth moved, but no sound came out.

"Look at him," Andrew blurted. "He's got stage fright."

"It's a fright, all right," Nina murmured. "But it has nothing to do with a stage."

The new ghost slowly floated through the air, straight to the items the kids had brought back from the Blackburn Estate. Her slender pale finger ran along the chip on the small dish. Finally, the strange ghost paused in front of the fiddle and smiled. She gently plucked three strings. They played the same tune Cassidy had heard when they left the Blackburn Estate. The notes seemed to bounce off the walls as the ghost floated over to stand beside Jeff. The ghost tilted her head, closed her eyes, and began to sing.

Her voice was high and loud. A good

dose of screeching was mixed in, though it sounded like it came from a different part of the room. . . .

Nina put her fingers in her ears. Cassidy covered her ears with her hands. Jeff stood at the front of the room and stared.

Of course, they were the only kids who saw or heard any of the ghostly antics.

"Don't you want to try out for the play?" Mr. Morton asked Jeff gently. "You don't have to if you don't want to. I can give the part to someone else."

That was enough to snap Jeff out of his stupor. He forgot all about ghosts and looked at his teacher. "Of course I want to try out," he said. "I'm perfect for this part."

Jeff tried to ignore the singing. . . . He concentrated on reading the lines for the play. "Arliss, you get out of that water," he began reading.

But the louder the new ghost sang, the

louder Jeff had to yell out his part. Soon, he was shouting so loudly the kids in the front row had to cover their ears. Carla and Darla giggled and Andrew laughed out loud.

"Thank you, Jeff," Mr. Morton finally said. "I think you've showed the rest of the class that you can project your voice so all can hear."

Jeff hung his head and walked back to his seat.

Just then Huxley, the ghost dog, appeared in the middle of the room and lifted his nose toward the bookshelves. He let out a howl that Cassidy was sure shook the walls. It was so loud, in fact, that it broke the ghost sound barrier. Everyone in the class could hear the ghostly howl. Mr. Morton stopped dead in his tracks. Carla and Darla screamed. Andrew fell to the ground and hid under his desk.

Mr. Morton wiped at his glasses until

he had two clear circles to see through. "What was that?" Mr. Morton gasped.

The room had suddenly grown quiet — very quiet. Cassidy, Nina, and Jeff looked around. That's when Jeff saw a tiny shadow huddled on the bookshelves.

"Oh, no," he muttered. "It can't be . . ."

"Is that what I think it is?" Nina whispered. . . .

Cassidy nodded. "It's a *ghost cat*!"

MEET
Geronimo Stilton

A REPORTER WITH A NOSE FOR GREAT STORIES

Who is Geronimo Stilton? Why, that's me! I run a newspaper, but my true passion is writing tales of adventure. Here on Mouse Island, my books are all bestsellers! What's that? You've never read one? Well, my books are full of fun. They are whisker-licking-good stories, and that's a promise!

www.scholastic.com/kids

THE SECRETS OF DROON

by TONY ABBOTT

A Hidden Door, A Magical Staircase. Discover the World of Droon!

Underneath the steps leading down to Eric's basement is a hidden storage space. It's dusty and old—nothing special at all. But when Eric, Julie, and Neal all huddle inside the gray room together, something unbelievable happens. A glittering light and then a rainbow-colored staircase appear. And as the kids take their very first step down into the mysterious land of Droon, they know that only magic and adventure await them!

**Play the Droon Castle Chase at
www.scholastic.com/droon**

Creepy, weird, wacky, and
funny things happen to
the Bailey School Kids!™
Collect and read them all!

The Adventures of
THE
BAILEY SCHOOL
KIDS®

The Adventures of THE BAILEY SCHOOL KIDS®

Available wherever you buy books, or use this order form

Scholastic Inc., P.O. Box 7502, Jefferson City, MO 65102

Please send me the books I have checked above. I am enclosing $_____ (please add $2.00 to cover shipping and
handling). Send check or money order — no cash or C.O.D.s please.

Name _____

Address _____

City_____ State/Zip _____

Please allow four to six weeks for delivery. Offer good in the U.S. only. Sorry, mail orders are not available to residents of
Canada. Prices subject to change.

BSK902